Keep in Touch

Letters, Notes, and More from

The Sisterhood of the Traveling Pants

Delacorte Press

Published by Delacorte Press, an imprint of Random House Children's Books,
a division of Random House, Inc., New York

Visit us on the Web! www.randomhouse.com/teens
Educators and librarians, for a variety of teaching tools, visit us at
www.randomhouse.com/teachers

Library of Congress Cataloging-in-Publication Data is available upon request.
ISBN: 0-553-37608-X (trade pbk.)
ISBN: 0-385-90943-8 (lib. bdg.)

Book design by Lauren Monchik

Printed in the United States of America

April 2005

10 9 8 7 6 5 4 3 2 1

BVG

Keep in Touch

Letters, Notes, and More from

The Sisterhood of the Traveling Pants

Books you may enjoy:

The Sisterhood of the Traveling Pants by Ann Brashares

The Second Summer of the Sisterhood by Ann Brashares

Girls in Pants by Ann Brashares

*The Sisterhood of the Traveling Pants:
The Official Scrapbook*

✢

Contents

Introduction

In our movie, *The Sisterhood of the Traveling Pants*, me (Carmen) and Bridget, Lena, and Tibby (my best friends since our mothers took a prenatal aerobics class the summer we were all born) spend our sixteenth summer apart. And even though we're all excited (except, understandably, for Tibby), it's still scary for four tighter-than-tight friends who are used to spending all their time together to be away from each another. Knowing us, you can only imagine how hard it is.

Here's what happens: Bridget's off to soccer camp in Baja California; Lena flies to Santorini, Greece, to visit her grandparents; Tibby's stuck in Bethesda, working as a discount store clerk at Wallman's; and I'm looking forward to some quality time with my dad in South Carolina (my parents divorced when I was little). But just because we're separated doesn't mean that we aren't thinking about each other. In fact, knowing that we have each other's backs makes the things we go through this summer (and boy, do we go through some *things*) much easier to deal with.

Of course, when you're like Bee (that's what we call Bridget sometimes), 3,000 miles away on a soccer field, or like Lena, hanging out with gorgeous Greek boys in beachside tavernas in Santorini, keeping in touch isn't just a matter of picking up the phone (especially since none of us has a cell phone or Blackberry or Palm). . . .

That's where the Pants come in.

The Traveling Pants are the magic fibers that hold our friendship together. Sharing the Pants is the way us girls stay connected over the summer—and the letters that each one of us writes when we FedEx the Pants to the next person express all the emotion that we feel.

In this movie companion book, you will be able to read some of the letters that we, the Sisterhood of the Traveling Pants, share over this incredible summer. But there are lots of other things that you'll be interested in too. You didn't think that the only time we wrote down our thoughts was when we FedExed the Pants, now, did you? Not only will you get a sneak peek into the letters and notes that we shared during this amazing summer, you can also read the (lame!) notes we wrote to each other—when we were eleven! Some stuff will make you laugh—like Bee's childhood birthday card. And some stuff will make you cry—like Tibby's list of things she hates about the hospital where Bailey is. At the end of this book, there's a special section that tells you all about how YOU can write the most amazing notes to your friends—in mere seconds. Keeping in touch with the people you love and who love you—now, what's more important than that?

A friendship can weather most things and thrive in thin soil; but it needs a little mulch of letters and phone calls and small, silly presents every so often—just to save it from drying out completely.

—Pam Brown

In case you're confused, here's a key to who wrote each item in this book— or who it is about. So, for example, when you see a star, you'll know that it's a Bridget entry.

★ **Bridget**

❀ *Carmen*

♥ lena

✳ tibby

♣ all the girls

B. & A. the P.

Before and After the Pants

The Very,
Very
beginning

Prenatal Aerobics

Class Roster:
Septembers

Kaligaris, Ariadne

Lowell, Christina

Tomko-Rollins, Alice

Vreeland, Marlene

HAppY 6TH BirTHday, CARMEN!
LOVe and KissiS,
BRIDGet (WHO IS STIL oldur THEN YOU)

A Ceramics Painting Party

**Join Lena as she celebrates her 8th birthday
with a work of art!
Party date: Saturday, August 29th, 1-4pm
Party place: Paint-N-Putter, 114 Sycamore Blvd.
RSVP by August 21st,
thekaligarisfamily@gateway.net**

So fun!

✳

If you like to have fun and you like to eat,
Tabitha's 8th birthday party will be a real treat!

The cooks at Classic Chef are ready and able
To help us make pizza and put it on the table!

Toques and aprons will be provided-
just bring your appetite!   Bacon, pepperoni, or sausage?

Saturday, 9/12, from 4-6 at Classic Chef.
Please RSVP to Alice Tomko-Rollins by August 30th

★

It's a swim party
for Bridget Vreeland's birthday!

Where: The Y

When: Sunday, September 13th

Time: 6–9

We hope you can make it!

✿

You're invited to a Saturday afternoon of pampering at

Carmen's Beautiful Birthday Bar!

Pink nail polish, French braids, and lotions and potions

are how we'll celebrate Carmen Lowell's turning eight!

Call Christina with regrets only.

❁
RAVE!

DAD and I had the best time today. The best! He was in DC just for the day, but we managed to squeeze in breakfast at Bagels + Lox (poppy bagel with veggie cream cheese and chocolate milk for me, everything bagel, toasted with butter, and iced green tea for him), and then we went to the FREDERICK LAW OLMSted exhibit at the Smithsonian. It was so cool! I wish we could spend more time together instead of having to cram Things in on the Spur of the moment. I miss him.

*

A TREATISE ON WHY I, TABITHA ROLLINS, SHOULD NOT BE
FORCED TO PLAY THE PICCOLO.

FIRSTLY, LET ME MAKE IT CLEAR THAT I REALIZE THAT THIS
IS AN UNORTHODOX REQUEST. BUT WE HAVE BEEN TOLD TO
STAND UP FOR OUR RIGHTS HERE AT SCHOOL, AND IF I AM
FORCED TO PLAY THE PICCOLO, MY RIGHTS WILL HAVE BEEN
VIOLATED.

FOURTH GRADE IS A TIME OF EXPLORATION. IT IS A TIME OF
LEARNING, A TIME OF WONDER, AND A TIME OF ENJOYING WHAT
IS LEFT OF CHILDHOOD. IT IS NOT A TIME OF PRACTICING AN
INSTRUMENT THAT WILL HAVE NO VIABLE PURPOSE AS A
CONTRIBUTING ADULT IN OUR SOCIETY.

I IMPLORE YOU—RESPECT MY RIGHTS AS A CITIZEN OF THIS
COMMUNITY, AND DO NOT MAKE ME A PICCOLO PLAYER AGAINST
MY WILL. A PICCOLO PLAYER COERCED TO PLAY THE PICCOLO
CANNOT MAKE MUSIC OF THE HEART.

ANY FURTHER QUESTIONS CAN BE ADDRESSED TO MY
ATTORNEYS, MR. & MRS. ROLLINS.

SINCERELY,
TABITHA ·TIBBY· ROLLINS

18

slumber party
pass-along note
written at
age 9

Answer, fold down the paper, and
pass it along. Do not read the
other answers!!!!

Q. If you could have anything in the
world, what would it be?

Peace on earth.

A LIFETIME SUPPLY OF FREE MOVIES FROM BLOCKBUSTER.

Being on the Olympic soccer team.

My mom and dad together again

Q. Do you think that you'll get it
one day?

I hope so.

YEAH, WITH POPCORN I BET.

Definitely!

Maybe...

19

Q. Would it make you happy?
Yes.
DUH!
Yes!
Very.

Q. What is your favorite subject?
Art.
MUSIC.
Gym.
Language Arts.

Q. What do you like to do after school?
Draw.
GO ONLINE.
Spend time with my friends.
Snack and watch TV.

Q. Have you ever kissed a boy?
No.
NO.

Yes. ☺
No.

Q. If not, is there a boy you
   really, really want to kiss?
   What???? When?????
   NOT REALLY, REALLY. BUT SORT OF.
   Last year! You knew that.
   Yes.

Q. If yes, do you want him to know?
   No way! (I should have answered yes above.)
   No.
   Sure!
   Maybe.

Q. Who is the cutest boy at our school?
   Chris Cascio.
   LUCAS MATHIAS.
   David Rosenberg.
   David???? Jesse Cartwright.

★

Bridget's Xmas List
Age 11

A puppy
SKECHERS
cleats
Soccer Starzz! mag. subscriptioN
Watch
Flying lessons
HolidaY BarbiE

❀

Carmen's Christmas Wish List
For Dad
Age 11

cell phone
Game Boy cartridges
A trip to THe place of Your
  choice! The zoo, DC landmaRks,
  Six Flags
JeaNS

❀

Carmen's Christmas Wish List
For Mom
Age 11

cell phone
diary
calendar (no characters, please)
red sweater
white sweATer
black Skirt
MAC lip gloss OR Lip Smackers
  (root beer flavor)
Chanel No. 5 Perfume
New beDDIng for my room
  (NOT pink)
JeanS

♥

Lena's Christmas List
Age 11

Faber-Castell watercolor pencils
Agatha Christie novels—any
Jeans

*

WHAT I WANT FOR CHRISTMAS

(TIBBY, AGE 11)

CELL PHONE

DISCMAN

BILLIE HOLIDAY, TORI AMOS, AND PRINCE CDS

STAR WARS DVDS (ANY)

SUEDE COWBOY HAT

BLACK LEATHER BELT (SIZE S)

JEANS

*

Mrs. McCready says we have to write a short biography on a royal family if we want extra credit. Here is mine.

The Royal Family of Rock.

King ... Elvis. That's easy.

Queen ... Hmmm. Christina? Latifah? The Jeopardy! theme music is playing . . . OKAY already. I'll go with Madonna since she's an icon and a mother. Plus she and Elvis could do a mean boogie.

Prince ... Prince ☺

Princess ... What about Gwen Stefani? She unequivocally looks the part plus she can really sing. And I bet she'd really and truly get along with Prince too, so the sibling rivalry should be minimal.

I realize I may not get full credit for this, seeing that it's a bit out of the box. But since Mrs. McCready is so COOL, maybe I'll get some.

★

GREAT NAMES FOR MY BAND

Vreeland
Security
Vocal Loco
The Cleats
All 4 You
Maryland
Proper Puppy
Thirteen
Meg

26

✿

Carmabelle: Dear Tibby (the TRAITOR),
that was SO not cool of you to not come
to my Halloween party. The whole point was
that we were supposed to be dressed up like Dorothy,
the Scarecrow, the Tin Man, and the Cowardly Lion,
and without you we looked dumb. Well, Lena looked
pretty as Dorothy. But Bee's stuffing kept

Carmabelle: falling out, and the silver paint I had on
my face started cracking and that was really itchy.
But ANYWAY. When you tell someone you are coming
to her party, you are SUPPOSED to come. You are NOT
supposed to go to another party (Jessica B. said she
thought she saw you outside Alexis's house at the
exact time you were supposed

Carmabelle: to be doing the Down the Yellow Brick
Road dance with us.) And you didn't even call to tell
me, you just didn't show up, which, in my humble
opinion, is a very cowardly thing to do.
Anyway, I just want you to know that you missed a
really

Carmabelle: great party. We wrapped each other up
like mummies, we played this game where you stick
your hand into a bowl of goop and try to guess what
it is, and we ate homemade donuts. And my mom and
I made up these really cool treat bags. I still have
yours. Though I really wanted to eat it. But Bridget
and Lena thought maybe you had a very,

Carmabelle: very good excuse.
You better.
Carmen

✳

Tibbywashere: Dear Miss Jump to
Conclusions: For your information, the
reason I did not come to your party
was that my mom had to trim the lion's
mane because it was in my face. Not only
did she trim the mane, she chopped off a huge hunk
of my hair. I looked horrific. There was no way I was
going out of the house looking like such a reject. I

Tibbywashere: don't know who Jessica saw but it
wasn't me. My mom tried calling you but no one
picked up.
Do you feel bad now?
Tibby

❁

Carmabelle: I am really sorry. Do you forgive me?
** Do you still look like a freak?

*

Tibbywashere:
Yes.
Yes.
But if you come over with the goodie bag, at least I'll
be a happy freak.
Tib

*

I know you're just trying to make me
feel better, Carma, but come ON!
What are they thinking having another
baby at their age? They're older than your
mom! They were born before the Internet. They are
ANCIENT!!! Ew, ew, and ew. What was I, just
some experiment from their hippie days and now it's
time to start their real family? This totally,
completely sucks.

And if they think I'm going to babysit these—
these—these CRETINS, they are out of their minds.

Tibby's note
to carmen.
age 13

Dear Tibby:

    I have so much to tell you, and
that is a really good thing. Ya
know why? Cuz it's National Letter
Writing Month! Did you know that there
was such a thing? Well, there is, and I
am going to take full advantage. My mom read about
it in one of her magazines. There are all sorts of
cool days and weeks to celebrate — like, for example,
National Puzzle Day, which also takes place during
January. Which got me thinking. Maybe you and Lena
and Bridget can come over Friday night and we can
do a puzzle. My mom and I never finished our
Christmas one. But I think that the manufacturer
left out some of the pieces. Anyway, do you want to
do that? And I can fill you in on what happened
between me and YOU KNOW WHO. When he walked by
me in the hall, he did that little shoulder thing. You
know, where he kind of shrugs and kind of glances
at me, which is his way of saying hello even if
Bridget doesn't buy it. So I did my version of saying
hello, which is turning up the corners of my mouth
ever so slightly and then readjusting my backpack so
it looks like I'm busy but not too busy to say hi.
What do you think it means? Do you think YOU KNOW
WHO (let's call him YKW) is going to ask me to the

Letter passed from
carmen to Tibby
in the hall.
age 13

winter formal? If he does I'm going to ask Lena if I can borrow that green dress she got at the mall that she never wears. It probably won't even fit me but maybe the gods will smile down on me. YKW looked so AMAZING today. He wore this Quiksilver shirt that fit him really good and a pair of faded jeans, and a puka shell necklace which could look really dorky on some people but not on YKW. Anyway, I was going—SHOOT! Mr. Callahan is giving me one of his famous dirty looks so I guess I better get back to writing down our bio lab homework. Ergh.

Carmen

**make sure you write back in January, hee hee!

*

Dear Carmen:

Didn't we just see each other in lunch an hour ago?

Tibby

ps Maybe he's shrugging because he has a tic.

Dear Girls:

It's me, your friendly neighborhood Carmen, writing to tell you of an awesome opportunity — it's Write a Novel Month! The entire month of November is devoted to coming up with an idea for a book and writing it. Get your pencils sharpened! I'm not sure if a month will be enough time since I don't have an idea yet. So I thought maybe you could help me. Here are the ideas I'm thinking of:

A girl, Carmella, meets a really hot boy and they fall in love, only to find out that the boy is really in the FBI's witness protection program. He's willing to give up everything, but saintlike Carmella tells him he must forget about her.

A boy finds out his father is a hit man and he has to decide whether or not to tell the authorities.

Twixie, a fairy, lives in an enchanted world of elves whose paradise is threatened by a mutinous group of gnomes.

Aliens take over Washington and no one can save the residents of our capital except a group of senior citizens from Florida who somehow have superhero powers (maybe it's something in the sun rays there???).

There isn't much time so write back and tell me what you think. I kind of like #1.

Carmen, Authoress

Letter from carmen to her friends. age 14

★

Dear Carmen:
   Uh, did someone spike your Halloween candy?
   Bridget

*

Dear Carmen:
   I would vote #2, except I think it should be about a girl who finds out her mother is the target of a hit person.
   Tibby

♥

Dear Carmen:
   I think they would all be great!
   Love,
   Lena

Letter Written to Bridget on the back of Tibby's English homework

*

Dear Bridget:

Carmen has just informed me that it's National TV Turnoff Week and that she is going to give up Passions. Like that's hard???? And I think the point is to turn off the TV for the whole week, not just one day. But anyway, I told her we would give her moral support and give up something too. I will give up Seinfeld reruns. You?

Tib

Dear Tibby:
Hmmm. No more CNN for me.
Bridget

Dear Bridget:
You are kidding, right? Right?
Tib

Dear Tibby:
You caught me. C-SPAN.
Bridget

Carmen gave her friends handmade cards on Valentine's Day.

Roses are Red
Violets are Blue
You guys are so great
I'm so glad I have you.
Happy Valentine's Day!

Tibby gave her friends each a copy of Francesca Lia Block's <u>Weetzie Bat</u> on Valentine's Day.

↓

*

This quote is in the book. Isn't it great?
"Love is a dangerous angel. . . . Especially nowadays."

♥

I love you!
Lena
↗
Lena gave her friends pink carnations on Valentine's Day.

★

Hope this makes you smile.
Best friends forever!
Bridget.
↗
Bridget gave her friends chocolate heart lollipops on Valentine's Day.

37

★

Dear Bridget & Family:
We are so sorry to hear of your loss.
Please know that you are in our thoughts
and prayers each and every day.
Sincerely,
The coaches and players
of the Bethesda Soccer League

G od, don't you love
to run?

—Bridget Vreeland

♥

Dear Mr. & and Mrs. Kaligaris:

What wonderful work Lena accomplished in Art Appreciation this past year. She was one of my finest students, and it was an honor to have her in class. I know she is off to Greece this summer, and I'd like you to encourage her to keep up with her sketch work. But in truth we don't need to tell her that. True artists observe the world around them as naturally as they breathe air.

Have a most enjoyable summer.

Sincerely,
Ms. A. Paulsen

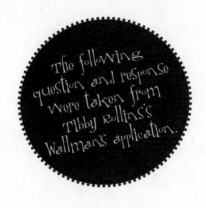

The following question and response were taken from Tibby Rollins's Wallman's application.

✳

7. Making our customers happy is our passion here at Wallman's! What is *your* passion (in 40 words or less)?

My passion is to work at Wallman's. It has been a passion of mine since, well, before I can remember. If I am hired, I guarantee I will be very, very passionate about my work.

(In the privacy of my own mind: I happen to need money to buy some new video equipment. And by the time I got around to looking for a job this summer, Wallman's was the only place hiring. Passion? Who are they kidding? On second thought—maybe they aren't kidding. Scary.)

❀

Must-Do Things in Charleston!

Eat at Chili's

Browse around City Market

Play at the Tennis Center

Rent as many DVDs as possible and make
   sure to stock up on Dad's favorite movie
   binge food item, Kit Kats!

Go to the Old Slave Mart Museum

Tan

Make arroz con pollo for Dad

Have something earth-shattering happen to
   me when I'm wearing the Pants—like meet
   Orlando Bloom!

Shop!

♥

Dear Bridget, Carmen, and Tibby,

I wanted to bring back each of you something special from my trip. If you could have anything from Greece, what would it be?

Love,

Lena

A Greek Boy

Olive oil for my mom and one of those T-shirts that says My Friend Went to Greece and All I Got Was This Lousy T-Shirt

Bootleg CDs

Dear Bridget, Carmen, and Tibby,

Okay, forget it. I'll surprise you.

Love,

Lena

Alice—
Tibby's mom—
handwritten
note

∗

Tibby—<u>Don't forget</u> to pick up an extra package of diapers at work today. Meredith is a size 3—and there's a coupon for Huggies on the counter. Dishes need to be loaded in the dishwasher, and there's at least 2 loads of sheets & towels piled up next to the washer. There's leftover pot roast in fridge for lunch if you want it. Have fun! Remember—DIAPERS!
Mom

This is a typed excerpt from carmen's prizewinning short story. "A cup of Joe."

❀

. . . And as she turned to him, she saw that his eyes were filled with something she couldn't name.

"Is there anything else?" she repeated, holding her hands up toward the ceiling.

He hesitated. "I—I guess not."

She knew, instinctively, that there was something unspoken between them. But she couldn't stay here any longer.

It was time to say good-bye.

Time to walk up to the next table and say, "Hello. Welcome to J&J's Diner. May I take your order, please?"

↑

She takes it in a folder to charleston to show her father. It never comes out of the folder.

♥

Things I'm going to draw this summer:
Various sculptures, statues, and assorted Greek
    items (vases?)
Café scenes
Churches
Papou and Yia-Yia's house

★

Dear Carma,

I've met some nice people here. You'd like them. Especially my new friend Diana. She's filled with energy and is really smart. Sound like anyone you know?

XO,
Bridget

*

A Note from Tibby about *Cinema*

Movies are made about many incredible things. One of them is keeping in touch with the friends you love. Here's the best of the best. No need to tell me if you find that some of them are cheesy. I make no excuses for my (excellent, I might add) taste.

You've Got Mail
   Joe (Tom Hanks) runs this bookstore chain that is taking business away from all the smaller stores, including a children's bookstore owned by Kathleen (Meg Ryan). They meet online and like each other, but in real life, they hate each other's guts. It's predictable, but it's still cute. And the store she worked at was cool. Way better than Wallman's. And New York City never looked so good.

The Shop Around the Corner

I never use the word *charming*, but I had to make an exception. James Stewart works in this little Budapest shop and wants a girlfriend. His coworker, Margaret Sullavan, is in the same boat (but for a boyfriend) and soon they become pen pals, but they don't know the true identity of said pen pals. Of course in real life they hate each other, but in letters, they fall in love. Sound familiar????? You've got to rent this one (and also to find out the ending, which I am not giving away for free here).

Now and Then

Back in the day before Demi Moore became Kutcherized, she made this flick about four childhood friends who grow up, grow apart, and then are all there when they really need each other. It's kind of like a girls' version of *Stand By Me* (which I watched again the other day and it is still good). Plus Christina Ricci and Janeane Garofalo are supremely awesome.

Igby Goes Down
   Igby is trying to find purpose in
his life, which is hard to do
considering his parents are nuts and he
is forced to go to these horrible
boarding schools. Then he meets Rachel
and Sookie and while you'd think things
would look down (considering Rachel's a
drug addict), Igby kind of goes up.
This one doesn't really fit into my
keeping in touch theme, but it's angsty
and confused and everything I would put
into a movie if I wasn't stuck doing a
suckumentary.

Divine Secrets of the Ya-Ya Sisterhood
   Okay, Rebecca Wells's book was way
better. But this movie isn't bad. I
liked Sidda and Vivi's relationship,
and the Ya-Ya Priestesses were really
kind of touching. Sandra Bullock is
almost as good as she was in *Speed*
(though no Keanu). Plus it has the word
Sisterhood in it.

Donnie Darko

I just love it, okay? While it won't really help you stay in touch with your friends, it does provide a good subject for conversation with them. Lena thinks it's a horror film. Bee says it's sci-fi, and Carmen refuses to watch it, despite the fact that Jake Gyllenhaal is the star. Can you believe her?

The DVD of *Laverne & Shirley,* the first season

Okay, I know I said *cinema*, but let's not be culture snobs here, all right? This is classic seventies TV—best-friendship at its best. Laverne De Fazio and Shirley Feeney are complete opposites—Laverne is sassy & brassy, Shirley is totally naïve—but they totally support and down deep love each other. They live in Milwaukee during the 1950s and work at a brewery. Priceless, huh? Their apartment is kind of threadbare but really homey. Shirley's boyfriend is named the Big Ragoo. (sp? Ragu?) Buy it now.

♥

Let's keep this <u>metaxi mas</u> (that's Greek for <u>between</u> <u>us</u>) so that a gazillion tourists won't overrun these places. . . .

The statues in the National Archaeological Museum

The cafés—and the barely drinkable (sorry, Yia-Yia) sludge the Greeks call coffee!

Afternoon naps—I think we should be able to do this on a regular basis in the United States. Kindergartners have naptime—and really, how tiring is putting on a paint smock or singing a song about the alphabet? Clearly, the Greeks are on to something here.

Tavernas (small restaurants run by Greek families). It is really neat to have our own family restaurant. There's always something good to eat. Like . . .

<u>pseftokeftedes</u>—yummy ball-thingies made with flour, tomato juice, spices, and veggies

<u>Ta Kavouraki</u>—the best wine (not that I had a full glass or anything)

Eggplant with feta and tomatoes, which is on practically every taverna menu in Greece

Get this—ricotta ice cream. Can you imagine how good this would taste with a slice of New York cheesecake?

♥

Dear T/B/C:

 Remember when Carmen used to tell us it was Pasta Day or World Turtle Day when we were kids? For some reason I kept thinking about that and it made me laugh. So in honor of Carmen's upcoming birthday, I have done some research. Did you know that National Watermelon Day is in August? Well, it is. And when I come home I want to sit down to a plateful of the red juicy stuff and have it dribble down my (tanned) chin. Yum. Okay, Tibby—tag, you're it!
 Lena

A Note from Tibby About Staying in Bethesda, Maryland, While Bridget, Carmen, and Lena (AKA Everyone Else) Go Away to Somewhere Fun

I'm trying not to be bitter about staying here in Bethesda, working at Wallman's, while my three best friends in the world are globe-trotting the planet.

Would I really want to be at a soccer camp in Baja? Nah. Too hot. Too many sweaty jocks. Not in possession of necessary athletic ability or fake ID to sneak across the Mexican border.

Would I really want to be in Charleston, SC? Uh-uhhh. Mm-mmm. I'd eat way too many bbq'd ribs and hushpuppies and shrimp po'boys, and then I'd come home, and I'd crave those foods, and we don't have that kind of good stuff in Bethesda, and then I'd need to go back to South Carolina which of course I couldn't afford with my meager Wallman's paycheck....

Would I really want to be in Santorini, Greece, gazing at the playground of Zeus and Athena instead of babysitting my little bro and sis? No way—oh, come on, who am I kidding??????

★

Dear Ma,

Soccer camp is SOOO much fun. The girls here are incredibly talented, and I'm learning more than I ever imagined possible. Did you know that Mia Hamm went here when she was a kid? At least that's what Diana (this really cool girl) told me, and Emily had heard the same thing too. They don't have Parents' Weekend here since the camp is kind of hard to get to, being in Baja and all. So you don't have to worry about not making it.

Ha ha. Are you laughing? I'm not. That wasn't a very funny joke. Good thing I'm not mailing this postcard.

Wish you were here more than you know,
Bridget

★

Dear Dad,
    Soccer camp is going well. The girls here
are nice, and I'm learning a lot.
    Love,
    Bridget

❀

RANT!

Don't think that I'm one of those self-absorbed kids who can't deal with her parents getting divorced. Been there, dealt with that. It happened when I was seven years old and I'm sixteen now. That was a whole lifetime ago. It was the worst thing in the world. But my friends helped me through it.

And I have no preconceived notions about stepparents. Ask anyone—I was totally the biggest Cinderella fan when I was in grade school. Did I let the wicked stepmother stop me? No. Did those nasty stepsisters ripping poor Cindy's dress to shreds scare me off? Nope. There was no reason to think that I'd be anything but nice and polite to any future steps of my own.

SO WHY DIDN'T MY DAD TELL ME HE WAS GETTING MARRIED? I mean, that is just SO uncool, unfair, unbelievable, unjust, and WRONG. You don't just invite your only daughter to visit you and be all "So how are you? What's going on? Oh, and by the way, I'm getting married." I can't believe he did that. I would have been able to handle it if he'd at least given me the courtesy of telling me like a normal person.

I would have.

And then right now loser krista has to go and tell me how Dad and Lydia met—he dialed the wrong number, Lydia picked up (which apparently is a miracle since he called at dinnertime—a SIN—and she

58

never answers the phone during dinner), and she agreed to meet him. At . . . a bowling alley. Apparently it was all one big happy bowlathon with Dad, Lydia, Krista, and oh yeah, Mr. Personality Plus, my soon-to-be stepbrother, Paul.

Too bad I missed it.

♥

Dear Tibby,

I think we might have been wrong about the Pants. The one time I wore them I almost drowned, and then got plucked onto a fishing boat by a guy who made me touch a live fish. So much for magic. At least I'm getting some good painting in. I love everything about this island except that you're not with me.

Infinite X's and O's,
Lenny

❀

A page from Lydia's journal . . .
The flowers are going to be gorgeous! Still debating on whether to wrap them in hand-tied bouquets or have the bridesmaids carry them in pomanders. . . .(I must remember to pick up the girls' shoes this week. Maybe they'll want to wear them around the house for a day to break them in? I don't want anyone falling down on the Big Day!)

*

Subjects for my documentary on lives of quiet desperation. Human existence at its lamest:

<u>Roberta</u> — Wallman's employee extraordinaire. Her serious gold-plated fingernails will look incredible on 10MM film.

<u>Duncan</u> — whoever made him manager knew what they were doing. He takes his job very seriously. I can't wait to make him look like the freak he is.

<u>Brenda</u> — waitress. Teased hair, major blue eye shadow. A chronic gum-snapper. The popping should add a little punch to things.

<u>Brian McBrian</u> — Bailey made a real find with BM. He's the undisputed King of the Quik-Mart Dragon Master. He's broken every record there is. Not that his name alone wasn't enough to put him on the list. If he isn't a loser, no one is.

❀

What Lydia wants to serve (probably) at the Wedding:

- Punch
- Cheese puffs
- Tiny hors d'oeuvres that you need to pop in your mouth in one gulp
- Tuna tartare
- Rubbery chicken with that sauce that every catering hall in America uses
- Green beans with slivered almonds
- Fingerling potatoes with fresh rosemary (that I know for sure. I heard her blabbing about it to Nancy on the phone.)
- 5-tiered cake with fresh flowers as the topper

What Dad would serve if he wasn't BRAINWASHED:

- Margaritas
- Tortilla chips and salsa
- Paella
- Sloppy Joes
- Potato salad
- Fresh fruit cobbler
- Chocolate cake

No. Wait a minute. That is what was served . . . when my dad married my mom.

Check, please.

Dear B/C/L:

You call that a challenge, Lena??? National Garage Sale Day is also in August. I'm gonna drag Bailey along with me and scavenge thru all the treasures. Maybe I'll score some vintage camera equipment. Or doilies. Bridget . . . ?

Tibby

✿

A page from Lydia's journal . . .

All right, Lydia, take a deep breath. There was a water main break in the hotel we chose for our wedding. The entire place is flooded, and the repairs won't be finished in time for our big day.

Luckily, my dear, sweet, amazing Al has stepped in and all the problems that seemed so insurmountable have been worked out. We have decided to have the wedding right here at home. After all, what is family without home? Our new caterer is wonderful, and the big day will surely be all we have dreamed about.

IM from Joe.
Paul's friend.
to Paul

GoForBroke: Dude!!! What happened to you after the game? You disappeared.

TheRodman: Al asked me to play tennis with his daughter.

GoForBroke: Is she hot???

TheRodman: Her name is Carmen. She's all right. She's got a wicked forehand.

✿

Cities I'd rather be in besides Charleston:

Baja

Santorini (technically, it's not really a city, is it?
  It's an island, right? Or is it a city and an
  island? Oh, who cares)

Bethesda. Yes, Bethesda.

Orlando. I could use a trip to Fantasyland right
  about now.

♥

He said the fight was about money and fish.
His grandfather says Papou cheated him.
Papou says his grandfather sold him bad fish.
Money and fish.
In a place like Ammoudi, that is everything.
But have you seen the Aegean Sea?
It is nothing at all.

67

*

Transcript of Tibby Rollins's first on-
camera interview with Brian McBrian,
King of the Quik-Mart Dragon Master,
assisted by me, Bailey Graffman.

   Tibby: Video arcade wizards are
fixtures at most convenience stores.
And Brian McBrian is a fixture at this
one. Dragon Master, he says, is his
"calling."

   Tibby: So, spend a lot of time here,
huh, Brian?

   Brian: Sometimes all day.

   Tibby: Wow, that's impressive. And
little things like school don't get in
the way?

   Brian: Not in the summer.

   Tibby: Ah. Good point. So,
essentially, you prefer to live it up
in a Quik-Mart instead of out there in
the real world.

   Bailey: (sorry, I had to insert
myself here.) Maybe he finds the Dragon
Master world more interesting. Tell us
about it, Brian.

Brian: Well, basically, you are Dirk the Daring in the year AD 1305. The goal? Rescue Princess Daphne, who's being guarded by Singe the Dragon. There's a total of twenty-eight chambers, with obstacles in each. Chamber One—the Snake Room. Snakes slither from the ceiling—you've got to chop them! But that's nothing compared to the Bubbling Ooze Room—you've got to chop the Bubbling Ooze Monster in half before he eats you. And that's a piece of cake compared to the rapids and whirlpools. . . . You don't actually confront the dragon until Chamber Twenty-three.

[Then Brian totally battled it out with a dragon. His hands were lightning fast on the knobs and buttons. It was amazing! And only after this epic battle was his warrior incinerated by dragon breath.]

Brian: Twenty-four. Only one person's ever made it all the way to Round Twenty-eight on this machine.

Tibby & Bailey: You?

Brian: (Nods) February 12th.

[At this point the video camera
started to beep. Tibby hadn't even
noticed!]

    Brian: Must have run out of tape.

    Tibby: Oh. Right.

    Bailey: What about the rest of the
interview?

    Tibby: We could always come back, I
guess. That okay with you?

    [That question was directed to
Brian. I knew she would come around.]

Mail day at for Cabin Four! Diana got a case of Snickers. Olivia got a huge box filled with granola bars, books, licorice, and a teddy bear with enough fluff to stuff my bed pillows. Sherrie got luv letters from her guy. And everyone in my cabin got tons of letters from god knows who. Wanna Know what I got?

Turn the page

★

Bridget:

    Have a good time. I will see you in August.

Dad

Movie Night with Krista

I suggest:
    Alien
She suggests:
    The Notebook

Trying again. I suggest:
    The Lord of the Rings
She suggests:
    Shall We Dance?

One more time. I suggest:
    Dumb and Dumber

She takes me up on it.

*

Dear Carmabelle,

I'm writing from the post office, and this Express Mail cost more than I make in two hours at Wallman's so the jeans better get to you tomorrow.

I'm sad to report that absolutely NOTHING of consequence happened to me while wearing the Pants. I spilled a Sprite, and Duncan, my pimple-faced manager, accused me of receipt withholding. (In pimple-faced manager lingo, that means forgetting to give the customer a sales slip.)

Other than that, the only thing I have to show for the Pants is the kid that delivered them. A wise-ass pain in the neck who's decided to permanently glue herself to my hip.

Too bad you can't Express Mail 12-year-olds.
Yours in Sisterhood,
Tibby

Dear Lena,

Kalemara! *Should I write this entire letter in Greek? Hi, honey. I'm sitting here at the kitchen table, drinking a cup of coffee, and missing you so much. I can't believe you've been in Greece for three weeks already! I am sure you are having a wonderful time. As many times as I have described it to you, you can't imagine what the caldera cliffs on Santorini look like until you see them, can you? Yia-Yia always said that Oia is the most beautiful village in Greece. Has she told you that? Well, now you know for yourself that it is true. Daddy and I wish we could be there with you, enjoying these months together. But we do not get the summer off as you do, lucky girl!*

We have been keeping busy. Dad has been putting in a lot of hours at the office and I have been working on the fund-raiser for church, redecorating the living room, and my volunteer work at the community center. Somehow the days just fly by. But the nights are much quieter without you here, and Dad and I keep talking about how soon you will be going off to college, and the house will be like a library!

Have you been able to visit the white sand beaches in Ammoudi, or the black sand one near the ruins at Akrotiri? I spent a lot of time there in my youth, and I can assure you, you can't go wrong with either one! Is Yia-Yia trying to fatten you up with her delicious cooking? Have you met all your cousins? How is your artwork coming along? We received the nicest note from your art teacher, Ms. Paulsen. She is very proud of you, as are we.

My Lena, please give Papou and Yia-Yia big hugs and kisses from me. I am sure you are doing this already, but please try to help them as much as you can—pick up after yourself, chip in with the cooking (if they will let you), do your laundry, et cetera. It has been many years since they had teenagers living in the house!
All my love,
Mom

＊

Dear T/C/L:
I asked my roommates if they knew of any holidays in August. They were all . . . "Huh??" Then I lucked out. It is National Inventors Month according to one of the camp cooks, an aspiring Bill Gates. I wish I could invent something—a soccer ball that always goes where you want it to. Or air-conditioned sneakers. Or zero-calorie Snickers bars. Gotta think about it. Carmen, backatcha.
Bridget

❀
RANT!

Do you know that Lydia doesn't wash her own sheets? Oh, no, no, no, no, <u>no</u>. She has MARIA do that. MARIA, the housekeeper. MARIA, whose "English isn't real good." Can you believe Lydia actually used those very words with me? Does she not REALIZE that I'm Hispanic? Does she not REALIZE how completely insensitive she is? You know, I don't think she doesis.

And while I'm at it, Krista has got to be the sorriest excuse for an American teenager on the planet. She's like this miniature version of her mom. Translation: her hair is Pam Anderson blond and she thinks Pepto-Bismol pink is a hot color. She and her mother are like the Sunshine Twins on uppers.

To: sugarandspiceandnutmegtoo.net
From: kristacool@cloud16.net
Re: Carmen

Things at my house are still not better. I am trying to be nice. But it is not easy. She doesn't seem like she wants to be friends. She's always scowling and stomping and slamming her bedroom door.

Today when she thought I wasn't looking she kept sneaking glances at my new pink Lilly Pulitzer sweater and matching bag that Mama bought me last week at Belks. Do you think I should offer to loan them to her? Maybe that would make her nicer to me.

I've been thinking. Do you think Carmen would help me write that Spanish paper? I've heard her say a few words and her accent sounds almost as good as Señorita Rosenblum.

To Whom It May Concern at
Sega:

   I'm writing to tell you
about a friend of mine, Brian
McBrian. He is a complete
genius at your game Dragon Master. It's
this really fun game where you are Dirk
the Daring in the year AD 1305 and
you're trying to rescue Princess Daphne,
who's being guarded by Singe the Dragon.
   Duh! I guess you know that
already!!!! Anyway, you know how there
are 28 chambers? Well, Brian made it ALL
THE WAY to 28 back in February. How many
people do you know who have done that?
Not to insult you or anything, but I bet
most of the people in your company can't
do it. It's really hard!!!
   Anyway, if you are ever doing a
national search for the best Dragon
Master players, you should definitely
give Brian a call. You can find him
most days at the Quik-Mart on Ninth
Street right here in Bethesda.

   ☺
   Your friend,
   Bailey Graffman

**If you ever need help figuring out a
problem with the game or coming up with
something new, I know he would help you
out!

79

A page from Lydia's journal . . .

My hairstylist, Rene, and I have finally settled on a style. I'm sworn to secrecy, but it should be stunning. Rene feels that it would be best for Krista and Carmen to wear their hair up, or at least pulled back. Buns? Braided twists? Maybe elegant chignons . . . exciting! Maybe the girls and I can look at hairstyle magazines later tonight. I really want to hear their opinions.

♥

Did you know that Greece is the most spectacular place on the planet? Everyone I meet tells me how lucky I am that our family is from Santorini, because it's the most beautiful island of them all (though Mykonos and Andros sound amazing too). The sky is always cerulean and the sea is bathtub warm. I wish you all could be here with me to see it for yourselves. Maybe we can come back for a graduation trip!

Oodles of love,
Lena

✿

A page from Lydia's journal . . .

Our day of beauty at Exhilarate is all in place for
Saturday, August 2. We'll spend the morning getting
shiatsu massages and sea kelp facials. Then we'll have a
delicious lunch (of course it's spa cuisine, can't have us
not fit in our dresses!), and the afternoon will be all
about manis and pedis. The polish color Krista and
Carmen will be wearing is . . . da da dum . . .
Albuquerque Mauve! It's kind of like raspberry sherbet.
Guess they like to fancy up the name!

＊

A Note from Tibby About Siblings

If you ever are walking past Baby Gap, and they have one of those huge colorful posters hanging up in the store window of a photograph of some adorable toddler dressed in coordinating hat/outfit/sunglasses/sandals ensemble, and you find yourself saying, "Ooh, how cute!" RUN, don't walk, to your bike/car/bus stop as fast as you can.

It's all a crock. Preschoolers really are not all that cute. They're not! Instead, they are covered with Cheerios, they need constant diaper changing, and you always have to worry that they are about to break something, scribble with unwashable marker on the walls, or fall down and be horribly scarred for eternity. And then, of course, if they get sick, you have to worry about them throwing up on your new hoodie, spewing baby germs everywhere, or lying on the couch turning their little brains into jelly by watching too many Barney videos.

Trust me. It is not fun.

What? What! Oh, great. Excuse me. Someone's 2-year-old arm is stuck in one of our Pottery Barn dining room chairs.

★

My fave things, B. Vreeland,
Age 21 (hee hee)

living and breathing soccer 24/7
Baja
today's scrimmage where I kicked total butt
piña coladas
my flannel sleeping bag
Burt's <u>Bees</u> lip balm (get it? Bees?)
soccer coaches named Eric

♥

Dear Carmen,

 I know I should be writing about how utterly gorgeous Santorini is, or how clear the Aegean looks right now, or how delicious the fortalia and keftedes and the chickpea salad and basically everything that Yia-Yia makes are, but all I can think about is Kostos. Today I was sitting outside this fish market, right in the center of town, sketching this tiny dilapidated church. But the whole time I was sketching, I was waiting for Kostos to arrive. And sure enough, up he pulled on his Vespa (he has this ice chest that he keeps his fish in and he went inside the market to sell it). And when he came out, he totally knew why I was there—to see him! But I acted like I wasn't (only who sits near a smelly fish market unless they're waiting for someone, right?). He looked at my drawing, and he said I was an artist. I told him that I would like to be, someday. And that you ☺ said I will be one.

 And then do you know what he told me? That his parents were married in the church I was sketching, and that they were killed in a car accident. He used to live in the United States, in Chicago, but he moved back here to live with his grandfather. Isn't that the saddest thing you've ever heard? All I could tell him was I'm sorry. Then he asked me why I was drawing the church. I hadn't really thought about it. But I told him the truth—that I liked that at first it just looks sort of forgotten. But then you realize there's something beautiful about it too. Kostos said I should finish the sketch. And then, you know me, I got all flustered, and said I had to go, that if my grandparents saw me with him . . . and you know what? He asked me if I was afraid of them, or afraid of something else? And if you could see the way he looked at me, it was like he was boring a hole straight into my heart.

He's right, Car. I am afraid. There's a part of me that wants to let him in, but then I feel myself put this wall up and I don't understand why.

Maybe that's what strikes me most about Kostos. That despite everything he's suffered, he can still look at life in the most uncomplicated way. I realize now that I've never known that kind of faith, and it makes me sad. Sad that people like Kostos and Bridget, who have lost everything, can still be open to love. While I, who've lost nothing, am not.

Write back soon and tell me this will all work out. I miss you.

XO,

Lena

PS: Guess what? Tell Bridget she was right about the beaches. I don't need all those bathing suits after all.

PPS: Kidding!

The 8 worst things about being in a wedding

1. You are forced to wear a lavender dress that the bride chooses—except she isn't the one wearing it. How much sense does that make? If your butt looks fat or your arms jiggle? Doesn't matter. Completely unflattering? Tough cookies. You have no say.

2. Hundreds of photographs will be taken of you wearing this monstrosity. And, you are expected to SMILE in these photographs.

3. You are at the bride's beck and call. If required, you may even have to help her and her ugly dress get inside a Lilliputian bathroom stall, a fate worse than death.

4. You don't get to sit with your friends at the reception. You have to sit with the bridal party. Bridal party. Is that an oxymoron or what?

5. You must participate in all wedding traditions—catching the bouquet, tapping your spoon on a glass so the happy couple can kiss, dancing the Hokey Pokey—no matter how much you hate them (couple/traditions), otherwise you will stand out as the Poor Sport and people will talk about you behind your back. (One bright spot—egging the groom on to smush the cake in the bride's face.)

6. You have to endure Lydia's constant wedding babble.

7. Your soon-to-be stepsister tells you, a Latina, that your Spanish accent is almost as good as that of her 60-year-old Jewish Spanish teacher when you return from a trial run at the hair salon.

8. You have to smile when all you feel like doing is crying. When you — AHHHH! A FedEx package was waiting for me on my bed. You know what that means!!!

Bridget's
handwritten
cantina
napkin

★

CALL ME
Bridget
555-457-9851 (Ollie's cell phone)

Bailey's favorite ice cream flavors:
 Cookies and cream
 Mint chocolate chip
 Orange Creamsicle
 Praline mixed with blueberries and a
   bunch of graham crackers
   (I haven't actually tried that one
   but Roberta from Wallman's said she
   made it up at the Sweet Shoppe,
   where she also works. It sounds
   good. I hope I get to stop by and
   try it someday.)

✿

A page from Lydia's journal . . .

It's hard to believe, but we are down to one last fitting—
this Friday at 4 p.m. Krista and Carmen will look
absolutely gorgeous in their dresses. I can't wait to see
them on our wedding day.

What am I going to do to occupy myself when it's all
over????

★

Dear Lenny,

When I got your letter I screamed for about ten minutes. So, you found a hottie after all, huh? Well, me too. His name is Eric. He's one of the coaches and 100% off-limits, but I don't care. I've never wanted anything this much in my entire life.

I'm still waiting for Alarmin' Carmen to send me the Pants. In the meantime, I'm throwing all my pent-up energy into soccer, although that only seems to get me into more trouble. What can I say? I'm OBSESSED. And as we all know, we obsessed girls can't be responsible for our actions.

Can we? ☺

YTNF,
Bee

Movie Night with Lydia + Al

I suggest:
    Kramer vs. Kramer
They suggest:
    The Wedding Planner

(Sighing). I suggest:
    How to Lose a Guy in Ten Days
They suggest:
    Four Weddings and a Funeral

(Sighing louder). I suggest:
    The War of the Roses
They suggest:
    When Harry Met Sally

I suggest Y Tu mamá también (English subtitles optional).
    Lydia gets a phone call from the new caterer. Urgent need to discuss cold vs. hot appetizers. Dad rushes to her aid.
    Paul comes home. Surprise! He offers to drive me to Blockbuster. Surprise! I go.

Movie Night with Lydia + Al becomes Movie Night with Paul.

I suggest: Shrek
He suggests: Act II tub of microwave popcorn to go with it.
    Phew.

FROM THE DESK OF DR. LAMBERT

Regarding Bridget Vreeland . . . teachers are right to be concerned . . . need to talk to Bridget's father about issues raised during psych. testing . . . possible after-school counseling? . . . single-minded to the point of recklessness . . . follow-up is necessary.

❤

Things I will never forget . . .

Oia sunsets

Grilled chicken and feta cheese salad at the beach taverna

Papou's crease-lined forehead

The salty smell of the sea wafting through my bedroom window when I wake up

Swimming in the afternoon

Kostos Dounas

Dear Bridget:

I guess I was kidding myself to think that when the Pants arrived, they'd make things better somehow. I don't blame them for what happened. But I do hope they bring you better luck than they did me. Even more than that, may they bring you good sense. Sounds boring, I know, but trust me, from recent experience, a little common sense is not such a bad thing, Bee. Wear them well.

    Love,

    Carmen

♥

Things I have drawn this summer:

Seagulls swooping over the harbor at Ammoudi

The view from my bedroom window

The courtyard of the church where Kostos's parents were married

An old Greek woman

Fishing boats

Fish

The Vespa

Half-full bottles of fragrant olive oil

The sculpted arms of a fisherman

The cliffs overlooking the Caldera

My cousins dancing

The famous Oia sunset, though I could never do it justice

Kostos's torso

Kostos's face

Kostos's eyes

Lena doesn't see Bridget's letter when it arrives with the Pants. Only when she is packing her bags in Santorini, getting ready to head home, does she spy it.

    . . . It happened just how I always imagined it would. So why do I feel this way, Lena? How can something that is supposed to make you feel so complete end up leaving you so empty? I just . . . I wish so much I could talk to my mom. I need her. And that scares me.

    I wish I could talk to you, Lena. I wish I could disappear, just float away to some place where nothing hurts anymore.

    Bridget

*

Things I hate about Bethesda Memorial Hospital

1. The cafeteria (this one requires subcategories):
   a. No Odwalla or Snapple. Only carbonated beverages—and they don't even taste right.
   b. It closes at seven.
   c. The wallpaper is silver and green. Not appetizing.
   d. Everyone in there looks worried.

2. The sad little flower arrangements that they have in the waiting room. Aren't waiting rooms supposed to cheer you up?

3. The parking garage is deserted. There's probably a mass murderer sitting in there behind a Honda waiting for his next victim.

4. The receptionists look at you with really sad eyes like they feel sorry for you but you know that they look that way at everyone, so how meaningful a gesture is that? It's not.

5. Bailey is there.

♥

Dear Tibby,

Kostos left today. And I told him that I loved him. My heart is too full to write about it just now. Sometimes it all still seems like a dream. And I wonder—did the Pants bring it to me? Or did they just give me the courage to find it on my own? Maybe I'll never know the answer to that question. But one thing's for sure: we were right all along, Tibby. Those Pants are magic. And I know if you let them, they'll bring you some magic too.

All my love,
Lena

Bridget's Rule #11:

In the event of an

emergency, the pants

automatically go to the

sister in need, regardless

of the schedule.

RAVE!

I like to think that Fate had a hand in what happened this summer. Perhaps it sensed that we needed something to hold on to, some little piece of faith or magic that we could count on, when everything else we believed in slowly slipped away. . . .

It would be easy to say that the Pants changed everything this summer. But looking back now, I see that our lives changed because they had to. And that the real magic of the Pants was in bearing witness to this, and in somehow holding us together when it seemed like nothing would ever be the same again.

Some things would never be. But as Lena and Bridget both said, we know now that no matter how far we travel on our own separate paths, somehow we will always find our way back to each other. And as Tibby said, with that, we could get through anything.

The Dos and Don'ts
of Keeping in Touch

The Dos and Don'ts of Keeping in Touch

Even if you don't have a magical pair of pants, there's absolutely no excuse for not keeping in touch with your friends. Maybe you have a special friend who moved far away. Maybe you have pals you only see occasionally. Maybe you have different friends for different social gatherings—your swim club buddies, your temple friends, your book club clique. No matter who they are—or how far away they live—they probably would like to hear from you.

It doesn't need to take much time to reach out to a friend. What's important is that your words be fun to read and capture someone's interest. Fun, interesting letters are usually read over and over again—so be careful not to write anything you could one day regret. Whether it takes five minutes or five hours to write, the best letter is one that is written from the heart.

Here are some fun ways to use the written word to make sure your friends know you care:

IMs

Nice for a quick hello, and it's fun to get a message from someone out of the blue. However, an IM does not take the place of an honest-to-goodness letter. Make sure that the screen ID of the person you're IMing isn't used by someone else—or you could wind up having a chat with your friend's annoying brother.

A Don't Note from
Tibby about IMs

Beware. Be very ware. One time
this guy in my class IM'd me for
ten minutes, asking me advice about this
girl. Except I wasn't the one he was chatting
with. Good old Alice (AKA Mom) was online.
Trust me. You do not want to have to explain
a booty call to your mother.

E-mail

The best way to get information out fast—and you can send photos along with your note, a nice plus. E-mail is fine for everyday use, but, it doesn't have lasting power. When you're twenty and feeling all nostalgic for your teen years, will leafing through the saved mail in your in box be very satisfying? And there are a number of pitfalls. Your important message could fall into your friend's spam filter. Sometimes people send e-mails when they are feeling emotional: angry, sad, lovesick. Remember: once you click on Send, it's out of your hands—and into thousands of potential in boxes—forever.

Writing letters? Good idea if you're Carmen. Sending e-mails? Nice of you. Touchy-feely stuff isn't really my thing.

I'm more about telling people how I feel rather than writing it all down. My words never come out on paper how I mean them to. If I ever have to write something important, maybe Carmen can be my ghostwriter. Because if I like a guy or feel bad about something or want to say thanks, I'd rather just tell you that instead of going all Hallmark. Of course, birthday cards are cool, and I loved getting mail at camp. But friendship cards? Or congratulations cards?? My advice? Just be a friend. Say "Way to go!" You'll save yourself the cash—and the time.

There's a much more fun-and easy-way to stay close to your bffs: sports. Shoot hoops together. Organize a game of tag football (and make sure to include the local hotties). Get all granola and go hiking. Head out to a soccer field and kick the ball around. Play tennis. Get a little crazy.

Notes (the folded up ten times into a tiny square kind):

When you've got to tell your best friends something right away—and you're in the middle of biology class. But remember: anything you write can be held against you, especially if snagged by your teacher or a classmate with a grudge.

Snail mail

Not exactly practical for up-to-the-minute news (*Can you believe she's dating him??? There's an awesome sale going on this weekend at Abercrombie! What time is Joey's party?*), but when you have the time, it's the absolute best way to share a piece of yourself with your friends, and give them something that they can hold on to and read again and again (provided that it's a *friendly* letter). It's an effort you'll be really glad you made.

The best letters:

Are handwritten. There's something about writing a letter by hand that tells the recipient he or she is special enough for you to take the time to write. Wedding invitations are almost always addressed by hand.

Diana, Princess of Wales, wrote all her thank-you notes by hand, making them that much more special.

Are legible. You don't have to have perfect penmanship, but your friend should be able to decipher what you have to say without calling in reinforcements (and think about it: do you want other people reading your personal message?).

Are creative! Plain old white paper and blue ink are okay—but how much more personal (i.e., fun to receive) will your letter be if you use colorful pens, stickers, photographs, and drawings?

When you want to do something out of the ordinary, write your friend a note on . . .

A leaf
Fabric
A CD
A map
Gift wrap
A lunch bag
A place mat from your favorite restaurant
A card you make yourself
An accordion-folded book of postcards
An envelope
A pair of pants ☺

You may need to have your letter weighed at the post office to see if it requires extra postage.

A Note from Bailey About Letter Boxes

A letter box is a box in which you keep the letters that mean the most to you. Mine used to be a plain shoe box, but now it's covered and lined with flowered wrapping paper. My mom has kept one for me since I was little. It's filled with cards she and my dad got when I was born, birthday cards, valentines, kindergarten graduation cards, Christmas cards. I'm really glad she kept this box. When I'm feeling sad, I get it out and look through the cards. I like the ones that people made themselves, and the ones that people took the time to write a little message on, even if it's just "You rock, Bailey! Happy 8th Birthday!" It's funny how a piece of paper with some words on it can cheer you up.

A Do & Don't Note from Lydia about Wedding Invitations

Addressing and assembling wedding invitations is a simple, yet highly important, task. Using high-quality stationery shows good taste as well as reflecting your personal care and thoughtfulness. Remember to avoid nicknames, abbreviations, and the phrase "and family." Dates of single guests should receive their own invitations; however, unmarried people who live together can receive a single invitation. Always use the full titles of medical doctors and military officers. When you assemble your invitations in the envelopes, the printed side should always face you. And, most importantly, don't forget to place a stamp on the response envelope.

A Do Note from Carmen
About Writing Instruments

When I write letters, notes, or entries in
my journal, I don't just use _any_ pen. It
has to be either an extra-fine-tip black
Sharpie or one of these black pens that
have black circles on the top of the cap. I
don't know who makes them but my mom
brings them home from her job at the law
office and they write really awesomely. I
also have this pen with aqua-colored water
inside and when you hold it to write, the
water moves and inside the water are tiny
sea horses and glitter. It doesn't write
for crap, but I got it when I was eight,
and call me sentimental but I still like to
use it. The thicker the nib (that's the part
at the tip of the pen), the cooler your print-
ing will look. A guy who works in a paper
supply store told me that once and it's
true.

Everyone likes to get mail from a friend. Now that you've finished *Keep in Touch*, a book that revolves around friendship—and maybe even have seen the movie of *The Sisterhood of the Traveling Pants* or read the amazing novel by Ann Brashares—you've got some extra time on your hands. So what are you waiting for? Grab some paper and a pen and write and tell your friends all about it!

The Sisterhood of the Traveling Pants

Once there was a pair of pants. Just an ordinary pair of jeans. But these pants, the Traveling Pants, went on to do great things. This is the story of the four friends—Lena, Tibby, Bridget, and Carmen— who made it possible.

Read the novel that started it all.

Available everywhere!

Turn the page for an excerpt. . . .

Luck never gives:

it only lends.

—Ancient chinese proverb

"Can you close that suitcase?" Tibby asked Carmen. "It's making me sick."

Carmen glanced at the structured canvas bag splayed wantonly in the middle of her bed. Suddenly she wished she had all-new underwear. Her best satin pair was sprouting tiny ropes of elastic from the waistband.

"It's making *me* sick," Lena said. "I haven't started packing. My flight's at seven."

Carmen flopped the top of the suitcase closed and sat down on the carpeted floor. She was working on removing navy-blue polish from her toenails.

"Lena, could you not say that word anymore?" Tibby asked, wilting a little on the edge of Carmen's bed. "It's making me sick."

"Which word?" Bridget asked. "Packing? Flight? Seven?"

Tibby considered. "All of them."

"Oh, Tibs," Carmen said, grabbing Tibby's foot from where she sat. "It's gonna be okay."

Tibby took her foot back. "It's gonna be okay for you. You're going away. You're going to eat barbecue all the time and light firecrackers and everything."

Tibby had nonsensical ideas about what people did in South Carolina, but Carmen knew not to argue with her.

Lena let out a little hum of sympathy.

Tibby turned on her. "Don't make that pity noise, Lena."

Lena cleared her throat. "I didn't," she said quickly, even though she had.

"Don't wallow," Bridget urged Tibby. "You're wallowing."

"No," Tibby shot back. She held up hands crossed at the wrist in a hex sign to ward off Bridget. "No pep talks. No fair. I only let you do pep talks when *you* need to feel better."

"I wasn't doing a pep talk," Bridget said defensively, even though she was.

Carmen made her wise eyebrows. "Hey, Tibs? Maybe if you're nasty enough, you won't miss us and we won't miss you."

"Carma!" Tibby shouted, getting to her feet and thrusting a stiff arm at Carmen. "I see through that! You're doing psychological analysis on me. No! No!"

Carmen's cheeks flushed. "I am not," she said quietly.

The three of them sat, scolded into silence.

"God, Tibby, what is anybody allowed to say?" Bridget asked.

Tibby thought about it. "You can say . . ." She glanced around the room. She had tears welling in her eyes, but Carmen knew she didn't want them to show. "You can say . . ." Her eyes lighted on the pair of pants folded on the top of a stack of clothes on Carmen's dresser. "You can say, 'Hey, Tibby, want those pants?'"

Carmen looked baffled. She capped the polish remover, walked over to her dresser, and held up the pants. Tibby usually liked clothes that were ugly or challenging. These were just jeans. "You mean these?" They were creased in three places from inattention.

Tibby nodded sullenly. "Those."

"You really want them?" Carmen didn't feel like mentioning that she was planning to throw them away. Bigger points if they mattered.

"Uh-huh."

Tibby was demanding a little display of unconditional love. Then again, it was her right. Three of them were flying off on big adventures the next day, and Tibby was launching her career at Wallman's in scenic Bethesda for five cents over minimum wage.

"Fine," Carmen said benevolently, handing them over.

Tibby absently hugged the pants, slightly deflated at getting her way so fast.

Lena studied them. "Are those the pants you got at the secondhand place next to Yes!?"

"Yes!" Carmen shouted back.

Tibby unfolded them. "They're great."

The pants suddenly looked different to Carmen. Now that somebody cared about them, they looked a little nicer.

"Don't you think you should try them on?" Lena

asked practically. "If they fit Carmen, they aren't going to fit you."

Carmen and Tibby both glared at Lena, not sure who should take more offense.

"What?" Bridget said, hopping to Lena's aid. "You guys have completely different builds. Is that not obvious?"

"Fine," Tibby said, glad to be huffy again.

Tibby pulled off her dilapidated brown cargo pants, revealing lavender cotton underwear. She turned her back to her friends for the sake of drama as she pulled on the pants. She zipped, buttoned, and turned around. "Ta-da!"

Lena studied her. "Wow."

"Tibs, you're such a babe," Bridget proclaimed.

Tibby tried not to let her smile get loose. She went over to the mirror and turned to the side. "You think they're good?"

"Are those really my pants?" Carmen asked.

Tibby had narrow hips and long legs for her small frame. The pants fell below her waist, hugging her hips intimately. They revealed a white strip of flat stomach, a nice inny belly button.

"You look like a girl," Bridget added.

Tibby didn't quarrel. She knew as well as anyone that she looked skinny and shapeless in the oversized pants she usually wore.

The pants bagged a little at her feet, but that worked for Tibby.

Suddenly Tibby looked unsure. "I don't know. Maybe

somebody else should try them." Slowly she unbuttoned and unzipped.

"Tibby, you are crazy," Carmen said. "Those pants are in love with you. They want you for your body and your mind." She couldn't help seeing the pants in a completely new way.

Tibby threw them at Lena. "Here. You go."

"Why? They're meant to be yours," Lena argued.

Tibby shrugged. "Just try them."

Carmen could see Lena glancing at the pants with a certain amount of interest. "Why not? Lena, try 'em."

Lena looked at the pants warily. She shed her own khakis and pulled them on. She made sure they were buttoned and sitting straight on her hips before she glanced in the mirror.

Bridget considered.

"Lenny, you make me sick," Tibby offered.

"Jesus, Lena," Carmen said. *Sorry, Jesus,* she added to herself reflexively.

"They're *nice pants,*" Lena said reverently, almost whispering.

They were used to Lena, but Carmen knew that to the rest of the world she was fairly stunning. She had Mediterranean skin that tanned well, straight, shiny dark hair, and wide eyes roughly the color of celery. Her face was so lovely, so delicately structured, it kind of gave Carmen a stomachache. Carmen once confessed her worry to Tibby that some movie director was going to spot Lena and take her away, and Tibby admitted she had worried the exact same thing. Particularly beautiful people were like particularly funny-looking people, though. Once you knew them you mostly forgot about it.

The pants clung to Lena's waist and followed the line of her hips. They held close to the shape of her thighs and fell exactly to the tops of her feet. When she took two steps forward, they appeared to hug each of her muscles as they shifted and moved. Carmen gazed in wonder at how different was their effect from Lena's bland uniform of J. Crew khakis.

"Very sexy," Bridget said.

Lena snatched another peek at the mirror. She always held herself in a slightly awkward way, with her neck pushed forward, when she looked in a mirror. She winced. "I think maybe they're too tight," she said.

"Are you joking?" Tibby barked. "They are beautiful. They look a million times better than those lame-o pants you usually wear."

Lena turned to Tibby. "Was that a compliment somewhere in there?"

"Seriously, you have to have them," Tibby said. "They're like . . . transforming."

Lena fiddled with the waistband. She was never comfortable talking about the way she looked.

"You are always beautiful," Carmen added. "But Tibby's right . . . you look . . . just . . . different."

Lena slid the pants off her hips. "Bee has to try them."

"I do?"

"You do," Lena confirmed.

"She's too tall for them," Tibby said.

"Just try," Lena said.

"I don't need any more jeans," Bridget said. "I have, like, nine pairs."

"What, are you scared of them?" Carmen taunted. Stupid dares like that always worked on Bridget.

Bridget grabbed them from Lena. She took off her dark indigo jeans, kicked them into a pile on the floor, and pulled on the pants. At first she tried to pull the pants way up on her waist, so they would be too short, but as soon as she let go, the pants settled gracefully on her hips.

"Doo-doo-doo-doo," Carmen sang, hitting the notes of the *Twilight Zone* theme.

Bridget turned around to look at her backside. "What?"

"They're not short; they're perfect," Lena said.

Tibby cocked her head, studying Bridget carefully. "You look almost . . . small, Bee. Not your usual Amazon."

"The insult parade marches on," Lena said, laughing.

Bridget was tall, with broad shoulders and long legs and big hands. It was easy to think she was a big person, but she was surprisingly narrow through her hips and waist.

"She's right," Carmen said. "The pants fit better than your usual ones."

Bridget switched her butt in front of the mirror. "These do look good," she said. "Wow. I think I may love them."

"You've got a great little butt," Carmen pointed out.

Tibby laughed. "That from the queen of butts." She got a troublemaking look in her eyes. "Hey. You know how we find out if these pants are truly magical?"

"How?" Carmen asked.

Tibby jiggled her foot in the air. "You try them on. I know they're yours and all, but I'm just saying, scientifically speaking, that it is impossible for these pants to fit you too."

Carmen chewed the inside of her cheek. "Are you casting aspersions on my butt?"

"Oh, Carma. You know I envy it. I just don't think these pants are going to fit over it," Tibby explained reasonably.

Bridget and Lena nodded.

Suddenly Carmen was afraid that the pants that hugged each of her friends' bodies with loving grace would not fit over her upper thighs. She wasn't really chubby, but she had inherited her backside directly from the Puerto Rican half of the family. It was very nicely shaped, and most days she felt proud of it, but here with these pants and her three little-assed friends, she didn't feel like standing out like the big fatso.

"Nah. I don't want them," Carmen said, standing up and getting ready to try to change the subject. Six eyes remained fixed on the pants.

"Yes," Bridget said. "You have to."

"Please, Carmen?" Lena asked.

She saw too much anticipation on her friends' faces to drop it without a fight. "Fine. Don't expect them to fit or anything. I'm sure they won't."

"Carmen, they're *your* pants," Bridget pointed out.

"Yeah, smarty, but I never tried them on before." Carmen said it with enough force to ward off further questions. She pulled off her black flares and pulled on the jeans. They didn't stop at her thighs. They went right up over her hips without complaint. She fastened them. "So?" She wasn't ready to venture a look in the mirror yet.

Nobody said anything.

"What?" Carmen felt cursed. "What? Are they that bad?" She found the courage to meet Tibby's eye. "What?"

"I . . . I just . . ." Tibby trailed off.

"Oh my," Lena said quietly.

Carmen winced and looked away. "I'll just take them off, and we'll pretend this never happened," she said, her cheeks flushing.

Bridget found words. "Carmen, that's not it at all! Look at yourself! You are a thing of beauty. You are a vision. You are a supermodel."

Carmen put her hand on her hip and made a sour face. "That I doubt."

"Seriously. Look at yourself," Lena ordered. "These are magic pants."

Carmen looked at herself. First from far away, then from up close. From the front and then the back.

The CD they'd been listening to ended, but nobody seemed to notice. The phone was ringing distantly, but nobody got up to get it. The normally busy street was silent.

Carmen finally let out her breath. "These are magic pants."

❀   ❀   ❀

It was Bridget's idea. The discovery of magical pants on such a day, right before their first summer apart, warranted a trip to Gilda's. Tibby got the food and picked up her movie camera, Carmen brought the bad eighties dance music, Lena supplied the atmospherics. Bridget brought the large-sized bobby pins and the Pants. They handled the parents issue in their usual way—Carmen told her mom she'd be at Lena's, Lena told her mom she'd be at Tibby's, Tibby told her mom she'd be at Bridget's, and Bridget asked her brother to tell her dad she'd be at Carmen's. Bridget spent so much time at her friends' houses, it was doubtful that Perry would pass on the message or that her father would think to be concerned, but it was part of the tradition.

They all met up again at the entrance on Wisconsin Avenue at nine forty-five. The place was dark and closed of course, which was where the bobby pins came in. They all watched breathlessly as Bridget expertly jimmied the lock. They'd done this at least once a year for the last three years, but the breaking-in part never got less exciting. Luckily, Gilda's security remained as lame as ever. What was there to steal anyway? Smelly blue mats? A box of rusty, mismatched free weights?

The lock clicked, the doorknob turned, and they all raced up the stairs to the second floor, purposefully revving up a little hysteria in the black stairwell. Lena set up the blankets and the candles. Tibby laid out the food—raw cookie dough from a refrigerated tube, strawberry Pop-Tarts with pink icing, the hard, deformed kind of cheese puffs, sour Gummi Worms, and a few bottles of Odwalla. Carmen set up the music, starting with an awful and ancient Paula Abdul tune, while Bridget leaped around in front of the mirrored wall.

"I think this was your mom's spot, Lenny," Bridget called, bouncing again and again on an indented floorboard.

"Funny," Lena said. There was a famous picture of the four moms in their eighties aerobics gear with their stomachs sticking out, and Lena's mom was by far the hugest. Lena weighed more at birth than Bridget and her brother, Perry, put together.

"Ready?" Carmen turned the music down and placed the Pants ceremonially in the middle of the blanket.

Lena was still lighting candles.

"Bee, come on," Carmen shouted at Bridget, who was laughing at herself in front of the mirror.

When they were all gathered and Bridget stopped aerobicizing, Carmen began. "On the last night before the diaspora"—she paused briefly so everyone could admire her use of the word—"we discovered some magic." She felt an itchy tingle in the arches of her feet. "Magic comes in many forms. Tonight it comes to us in a pair of pants. I hereby propose that these Pants belong to us equally, that they will travel to all the places we're going, and they will keep us together when we are apart."

"Let's take the vow of the Traveling Pants." Bridget excitedly grabbed Lena's and Tibby's hands. Bridget and Carmen were always the ones who staged friendship ceremonies unabashedly. Tibby and Lena were the ones who acted like there was a camera crew in the room.

"Tonight we are Sisters of the Pants," Bridget intoned when they'd formed a ring. "Tonight we give the Pants the love of our Sisterhood so we can take that love wherever we go."

The candles flickered in the big, high-ceilinged room.

Lena looked solemn. Tibby's face showed that she was struggling, but Carmen couldn't tell whether it was against laughter or tears.

"We should write down the rules," Lena suggested. "So we know what to do with them—you know, like who gets them when."

They all agreed, so Bridget stole a piece of Gilda's stationery and a pen from the little office.

They ate snacks, and Tibby filmed for posterity, while they constructed the rules. The Manifesto, as Carmen called it. "I feel like a founding father," she said importantly. Lena was nominated to write it, because she had the best handwriting.

The rules took a while to sort out. Lena and Carmen wanted to focus on friendship-type rules, stuff about keeping in touch with one another over the summer, and making sure the Pants kept moving from one girl to the next. Tibby preferred to focus on random things you could and couldn't do in the Pants—like picking your nose. Bridget had the idea of inscribing the Pants with memories of the summer once they were all together again. By the time they'd agreed on ten rules, Lena held a motley list that ranged from sincere to silly. Carmen knew they would stick to them.

Next, they talked about how long each of them should have the Pants before passing them on, finally deciding that each person should send them on when she felt the time was right. But to keep the Pants moving, no one should keep them for over a week unless she really needed to. This meant that the Pants could possibly make the rounds twice before the end of the summer.

"Lena should have them first," Bridget said, tying two Gummi Worms together and biting off the sticky knot. "Greece is a good place to start."

"Can it be me next?" Tibby asked. "I'll be the one needing them to pull me out of my depression." Lena nodded sympathetically.

After that would be Carmen. Then Bridget. Then, just to mix things up, the Pants would bounce back in the opposite direction. From Bridget to Carmen to Tibby and back to Lena.

As they talked, midnight came to divide their last day together from their first day apart. There was a thrill in the air, and Carmen could see from her friends' faces that she wasn't the only one who felt it. The Pants seemed to be infused with the promises of the summer. This would be Carmen's first whole summer with her dad since she was a kid. She could picture herself with him, laughing it up, making him laugh, wearing the Pants.

In solemnity Lena laid the manifesto on top of the

Pants. Bridget called for a moment of silence. "To honor the Pants," she said.

"And the Sisterhood," Lena added.

Carmen felt tiny bumps rising along her arms. "And this moment. And this summer. And the rest of our lives."

"Together and apart," Tibby finished.